A Child is Born

Translated by Polly Lawson
First published in German as *Ein Kind ist geboren ...*
© 1984 bohem press, Zürich, Switzerland
English version © 2000 by Floris Books, 15 Harrison Gardens, Edinburgh
British Library CIP Data available
ISBN 0-86315-332-1
Printed in Italy

A Child is Born

A Christmas Story
Illustrated by Jindra Capek

Floris Books

Many years ago, one starry night in the heart of winter, the land lay frozen under a thick layer of snow.

Three travellers came to a poor shepherd's hut. Tired, cold, and seeking shelter, they called out and knocked on the door.

The young shepherd Jorim welcomed the strangers to the warm fire inside.

"I have very little," he said, "but you may share my simple meal."

He saw from their clothes that they came from a far Eastern land, and he began to wonder who they were.

As they ate together, the strangers began to tell their story.

"We are three star-gazers and we have travelled far, following a bright star. The star tells us a child is born, a king who will rule the world through love. The journey is long and hard, but we want to find and greet the new king."

Early next morning the three took their farewell, and the star led them on.

Jorim was deeply moved by what he had heard. A child who would change the world?

A king who would rule through love? In his heart the wish grew to follow the strangers on their journey.

"I, too, must greet this child, and the star will lead me," he declared.

He hurried to the village to tell everyone about the travellers. He wanted to share the wonderful news.

"The villagers have such a hard life," he said to himself. "They will be full of joy when they hear what I have to tell them."

Great excitement filled the hearts of the villagers when they heard the news about the child. They forgot their worries and began to sing and dance.

"Take this flute as a gift to the child," they said in farewell. "Let its music lighten the heart of everyone you meet, as well as the child. Tell him of us, and carry our hopes to him."

Jorim set out, following the star which still shone brightly, day and night. He told his story to everyone he met, and often they would laugh at him. But still he believed and carried on his journey.

One day, his path took him past a cottage where an old man was chopping logs. Jorim stopped to help, and soon there was enough firewood to last till spring.

"Where are you travelling in the midst of winter?" asked the old man when they had finished.

Jorim told him of the child who was to be born and the hope he carried with him.

"The nights are hard," said the old man. "I have little to offer, but take this woollen blanket as a gift to keep the child warm. It will protect you on your journey. And give the child my greetings, too."

As Jorim carried on his way,
following the star, he met a little girl
who was sitting beneath a tree, crying.

"What troubles you?" he asked.

"I lost my way and now I am too tired to
walk another step in the deep snow. But I
must reach home before dark."

Jorim helped the girl to her feet and com-
forted her.

"We shall find your way home together,"
he said, holding her hand.

As night was falling they reached the girl's home where the mother welcomed them gratefully.

Jorim told them the story of the three star-gazers and the new-born child who was to help all mankind.

The girl's mother said, "We are poor, but take this bread as a gift to the child. Tell him we, too, are waiting for him to be our king."

And Jorim went on his way.

Even now, Jorim sometimes had doubts
as he travelled on. If the star-gazers were
wrong, what should he tell all the people on
his way back?

Then at last the star stopped above a
humble stable, filling it with light.

"How can this be the birthplace of a
king?" he wondered.

Great joy was in Jorim's heart. There in the stable were the three star-gazers. Next to them a woman held a child in her arms.

Jorim took the blanket and wrapped it round the mother and child to keep them warm.

He gave the bread to be shared.

Then taking his flute he played a tune which sang of the life of poor people all over the world, their needs, their troubles, and above all, their hopes for the rule of the new-born king.